I Can Fly a Kite

An Ivy and Mack story

Written by Rebecca Colby

Illustrated by Gustavo Mazali

Collins

What's in this story?

Listen and say

Download the audio at www.collins.co.uk/839823

lion

dragon

elephant

kites

🎧 Ivy and Mack were in the garden. They saw a kite.

"I want a kite!" said Mack.

"Me too!" said Ivy. "Let's ask Dad."

4

Dad was in the kitchen. He smiled at Mack and Ivy. "What are you two doing?"

"Dad! Dad!" said Mack. "Can you get us a kite, please?"

"Yes. Can you, Dad?" asked Ivy. "Please?"

"I know. Let's *make* a kite," said Dad.
"It's more fun. And it's not difficult."
"What do we need?" asked Ivy.
Dad showed them on his computer.

They needed paper, wood, string, tape and scissors.

"You find the paper, Mack," said Ivy. "I can get the other things."

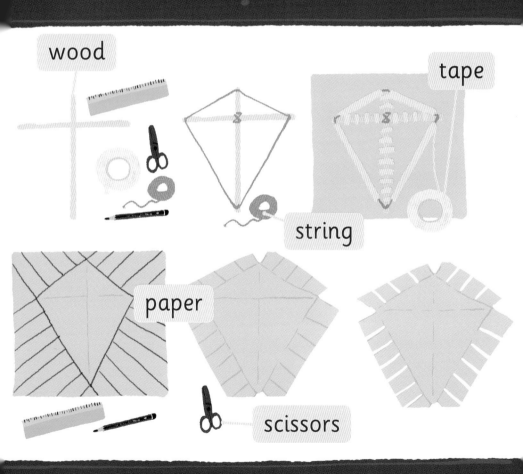

wood

tape

string

paper

scissors

Mack got the paper and put it on the table.

"We can make a bird kite," he said. "Or we can make a crocodile kite!"

Dad drew a picture on the paper.

"It's a dragon!" said Mack. "I love it!"

"So do I!" said Ivy. "We can colour it. Let's start."

Mack held the kite string. He ran in a straight line.

"I can fly a kite!" he said. "It's easy."

The kite was on the ground.
Ivy looked at it.

"No, you can't," she said. "It doesn't fly."

"What's wrong with our kite?"
asked Mack.

Ivy looked at the kite. "Look at the tail," she said. "We need to fix it."

They went back in the house.

Ivy took some more string and fixed the tail. She made it longer and better than before.

"Hooray!" said Mack. "It's new again."

Ivy ran with the kite.

"I can fly a kite!" she said. "It's easy!"

"No, you can't," said Mack. "It's in the tree, now!"

"What can we do?" asked Ivy. "The kite isn't moving."

"I have an idea!" said Mack.

Mack threw Croc up into the tree.
"What are you doing?" asked Ivy.
"I'm getting the kite down," said Mack.

The kite fell to the ground. Ivy laughed. "You did it!" she said. "You're the best brother, Mack."

Ivy and Mack held the kite. The wind carried it up. The kite flew up in the sky.

"Look! Look! It's flying!" said Ivy.

"We can fly a kite!" said Mack.

Ivy and Mack showed their kite to their cousins, Luke and Emma.

"I would like a kite, too," said Luke.

"Me too," said Emma.

"Let's make more kites," said Mack.

Everyone made a kite.

"My kite has a lion," said Luke.

"Mine has an elephant," said Emma.

"Mine has Croc on it," said Mack. "And Ivy's kite has Banjo the dog."

At the park, the children flew their kites.
They watched them go up into the sky
and dance in the wind.

Picture dictionary

Listen and repeat

ground

kite

sky

tail

wind

1 Look and order the story

2 Listen and say

Collins

Published by Collins
An imprint of HarperCollins*Publishers*
Westerhill Road
Bishopbriggs
Glasgow
G64 2QT

HarperCollins*Publishers*
1st Floor, Watermarque Building
Ringsend Road
Dublin 4
Ireland

William Collins' dream of knowledge for all began with the publication of his first book in 1819.

A self-educated mill worker, he not only enriched millions of lives, but also founded a flourishing publishing house. Today, staying true to this spirit, Collins books are packed with inspiration, innovation and practical expertise. They place you at the centre of a world of possibility and give you exactly what you need to explore it.

© HarperCollins*Publishers* Limited 2020

10 9 8 7 6 5 4 3 2

ISBN 978-0-00-839823-1

Collins® and COBUILD® are registered trademarks of HarperCollins*Publishers* Limited

www.collins.co.uk/elt

British Library Cataloguing in Publication Data

A catalogue record for this publication is available from the British Library.

Author: Rebecca Colby
Illustrator: Gustavo Mazali (Beehive)
Series editor: Rebecca Adlard
Publishing manager: Lisa Todd
Product managers: Jennifer Hall and Caroline Green
In-house editor: Alma Puts Keren
Project manager: Emily Hooton
Editor: Deborah Friedland
Proofreaders: Natalie Murray and Michael Lamb
Cover designer: Kevin Robbins
Typesetter: 2Hoots Publishing Services Ltd
Audio produced by id audio, London
Reading guide author: Julie Penn
Production controller: Rachel Weaver
Printed and bound by: GPS Group, Slovenia

MIX
Paper from
responsible sources

FSC
www.fsc.org

FSC™ C007454

This book is produced from independently certified FSC™ paper to ensure responsible forest management.

For more information visit: **www.harpercollins.co.uk/green**

Download the audio for this book and a reading guide for parents and teachers at www.collins.co.uk/839823